FIVE EXTRAORDINARY PARKER STORIES!

by **Parker Curry & Jessica Curry**
illustrated by **Brittany Jackson & Tajaé Keith**

Ready-to-Read

Simon Spotlight

New York   London   Toronto   Sydney   New Delhi

INCLUDES:
PARKER DRESSES UP
YOUR FRIEND, PARKER
PARKER GROWS A GARDEN
PARKER'S BIG FEELINGS
PARKER'S SLUMBER PARTY

SIMON SPOTLIGHT
An imprint of Simon & Schuster Children's Publishing Division
1230 Avenue of the Americas, New York, New York 10020
This Simon Spotlight paperback edition December 2024
Parker Dresses Up and *Your Friend, Parker* text copyright © 2022 by Parker Curry and Jessica Curry;
cover illustrations copyright © 2021, 2022 by Brittany Jackson;
interior illustrations copyright © 2022 by Brittany Jackson
Parker Grows a Garden text copyright © 2022 by Parker Curry and Jessica Curry;
illustrations copyright © 2022 by Brittany Jackson
Parker's Big Feelings text copyright © 2023 by Parker Curry and Jessica Curry;
illustrations copyright © 2023 by Brittany Jackson
Parker's Slumber Party text copyright © 2024 by Parker Curry and Jessica Curry;
illustrations copyright © 2024 by Brittany Jackson
All rights reserved, including the right of reproduction in whole or in part in any form.
SIMON SPOTLIGHT, READY-TO-READ, and colophon are registered trademarks
of Simon & Schuster, LLC.
Simon & Schuster: Celebrating 100 Years of Publishing in 2024
For information about special discounts for bulk purchases, please contact
Simon & Schuster Special Sales at 1-866-506-1949 or business@simonandschuster.com.
The Simon & Schuster Speakers Bureau can bring authors to your live event. For more information or to
book an event contact the Simon & Schuster Speakers Bureau at 1-866-248-3049 or visit our website
at www.simonspeakers.com.
Manufactured in China 0824 SCP
2 4 6 8 10 9 7 5 3 1
ISBN 978-1-6659-6322-0 (pbk)
ISBN 978-1-6659-0257-1 (*Parker Dresses Up* ebook)
ISBN 978-1-6659-0260-1 (*Your Friend, Parker* ebook)
ISBN 978-1-6659-3104-5 (*Parker Grows a Garden* ebook)
ISBN 978-1-6659-4277-5 (*Parker's Big Feelings* ebook)
ISBN 978-1-6659-4280-5 (*Parker's Slumber Party* ebook)
These titles were previously published individually
by Simon Spotlight with slightly different text and art.

PARKER DRESSES UP

My name is Parker.
I love to play outside.
But today it is raining.

Then I get an idea.
I can play dress-up!

My little sister and brother want to play too.

"I am a queen!"
says Ava.
Cash waves a magic wand.

I pull on a tutu.

Then I close my eyes.

I pretend I am a ballerina. "Bravo!" cheers the crowd.

Next I put on
a white coat.

I pretend
I am a doctor.
I can make anyone
feel better!

Then I hear a screech.
"No, Cash!" yells Ava.
"Cooks do not use hoses!"

The hose lands on my doll.
"Hey!" I yell.

Cash starts to cry.

My mom enters the room.
"What is wrong?"
she asks.

"Cooks do not use hoses," Ava says.

"Firefighters do not bother doctors," I say.

"Can a cook also be a firefighter?" my mom asks Ava.

Then she asks me, "Can a doctor also be a forgiving sister?"

"Everyone can be more than one thing," my mom says.

"Just look at me!
I am a mom and a writer."

"Look!" Cash says.
He is wearing
a new costume.

Now he is a superhero builder!

I put on a new costume too.
I dress up as
a mermaid teacher.

Ava dresses up as a fairy artist.

"Playing dress-up is the best thing in the world!" Ava says.

"President Parker does not agree," I say.

MAKING FASHION WAVES

Do you like playing dress-up like Parker? What are your favorite clothes and costumes to wear? Here are a few people who grew up to become famous fashion designers.

TRACY REESE is an American fashion designer who started her own clothing label in 1998. Many people have worn her designs, including Oprah Winfrey, Tracee Ellis Ross, Meghan Markle, and Michelle Obama! In 2019, Tracy created Hope for Flowers. The clothes in the Hope for Flowers line use sustainable materials that are better for the environment.

CHRISTOPHER JOHN ROGERS is an American fashion designer. Although he's still at the beginning of his career, he has already won many major awards! He also designed the outfit Vice President Kamala Harris wore on Inauguration Day when she was sworn in as the first Black American, the first South Asian American, and the first woman vice president of the United States of America.

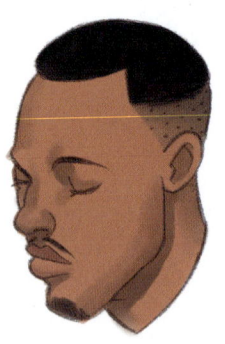

STELLA JEAN (say: JOHN) was born in Rome, Italy. She was a model before becoming a fashion designer. Stella tried out twice for a famous Italian fashion contest, but she was rejected both times. She didn't give up, though. On her third try, she won second place. Many of Stella's designs are inspired by her Haitian and Italian background.

If you could design new clothes or accessories, what would they look like? Try drawing your ideas in a sketchbook!

YOUR FRIEND, PARKER

My name is Parker.
This is my friend Gia.

We like dancing, drawing, and eating ice cream.

We do everything together!

Today my family is leaving for a road trip.

"Can Gia come too?"
I ask.
My mom shakes her head.

I wave goodbye to Gia.
I will miss her so much!

Dear Gia,
We are in North Carolina!

Today we went to the beach with Papi and Nana.

I built a sandcastle.
It was almost taller
than you and me!

Then we ate lobsters for dinner. Yum!

Dear Gia,
We are in Georgia!
Today we went to
an aquarium.

I saw many jellyfish dancing together. I named one Parker and another one Gia.

Later
we bought peaches
at the market.

I wish I could send one to you.

Dear Gia,
Remember when we went sledding?

Today I went sledding, but not in the snow.

It was in a sand dune in New Mexico!

My sled was
our favorite colors!

I drew a picture on my lantern.

I put a secret message on it too.
Do you want to know what it said?

It said, "I wish for Gia and me to be best friends forever!"

Then I watched the lantern float up to the sky.

You are a great friend.
Please write back soon!

Love, your friend,
Parker

A FRIENDSHIP OF TWO WRITERS

Just like Parker and Gia, **ZORA NEALE HURSTON** and **DOROTHY WEST** were two friends who enjoyed writing letters to each other.

Zora (1891–1960) and Dorothy (1907–1998) first became friends in New York City. They were both writers and members of the Harlem Renaissance (say: REH-nuh-sonts), a cultural movement that celebrated African American arts and politics.

In the 1920s, Zora traveled to gather stories about African American folklore in the South. During her trips, the two friends wrote postcards and letters to each other. They also sent gifts like books and pecans.

Zora and Dorothy were far apart, but they stayed friends by doing what they both loved: writing. They even lived together after Zora returned to New York City.

You can write a letter to a friend or family member too. Draw a picture or add stickers to make it fun. Make sure to sign your name at the bottom!

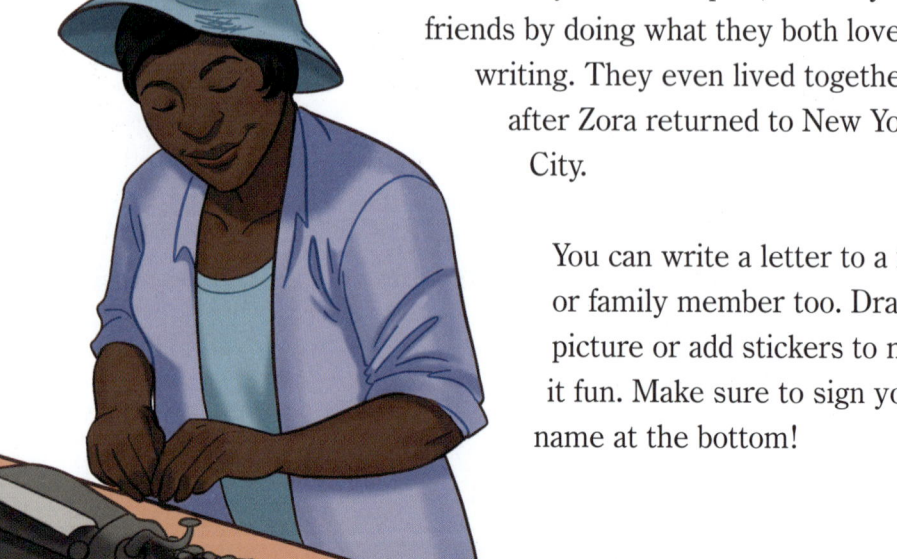

PARKER GROWS A GARDEN

My name is Parker.
I am visiting
my nana today.

Nana loves growing flowers in her garden. Now I am almost as tall as her rosebush.

I wish I could have my own garden too. "Wonderful idea!" my mom says.

I find a sunny spot
in my backyard.

My family helps prepare the soil.

In the fall Nana brings a tray of tulip bulbs.

We dig holes
and plant them
in the soil.

"Bulbs need water to grow roots," says Nana.

She gives me
a shiny watering can.

Nana says my garden will bloom in the spring.

I wait and wait and wait.

While I wait,
I draw pictures
of my tulip garden.

Pink tulips are my favorite!

When the snow melts, Mom Mom visits.

She helps me plant cucumbers and herbs.

"Look! A worm!"
I shout.

"Worms are important for healthy soil," my grandma explains.

One sunny day
I finally see green shoots
and leafy vines
poking out of the ground!

Soon my garden blooms!
I spy hummingbirds.

I smell the herbs . . .

but not before
I check for bees!

We invite my grandmas for a special dinner.

"These cucumbers are so crunchy!" says Nana.

"And the tulips are as pretty as Parker!" adds Mom Mom.

I love my grandmas!

And I love my garden!

GOING ON A NATURE WALK

Parker loves taking nature walks to see what is blooming in her neighborhood.

In the spring Parker looks forward to the cherry blossom trees. When the wind blows, cherry blossom petals rain down on her head!

In the summer Parker sees many different colors of hydrangea flowers. In the fall she sees squirrels gathering acorns. In the winter she looks for holly trees.

Nature walks are a fun way to spend time with family and friends. Wherever you live, there is always something new to discover outside!

PARKER'S BIG FEELINGS

My name is Parker.
I am the new kid in school.

Today our teacher says, "Pick a partner."

At lunch I spill juice on my new shirt.

At recess I fall
on the playground.
I wish this day was over!

When I get home I grab the book Gia and I are reading. Then I find a quiet spot.

"Is everything okay, Parker?" Mom asks.

"I miss Gia! I miss Papi! I miss my old school!" I cry.

"Those are big feelings," says Mom.

We write a list of things I can do to feel better.

I close my eyes.
I breathe in.
I pretend I am smelling a flower as I count to five.

1. Breathe

Now I breathe out.
I pretend I am blowing
out a candle.

Wow! I am feeling better!

2.Exercise

"Exercising helps turn on happy feelings,"
says Mom.
I put on my bike helmet.

I ride up and down the block! Whee!

"Parker needs time alone," Mom tells Ava and Cash.

We set up a reading nook with an owl timer!

When the timer hoots
I ask Ava and Cash,
"Want to play?"
"Yes!" they shout.

"Are you feeling better?" asks Mom.
You bet!

BIG HELP FOR BIG FEELINGS!

In this book, Parker's day is not going very well. She deals with lots of big feelings. Have you ever experienced big feelings like sadness, anger, jealousy, frustration, disappointment, or fear? Everyone feels those emotions at some point or another.

Sometimes it can seem like those feelings are here to stay. But big feelings don't last forever. There are even some things you can do to help yourself feel better.

Parker's mom helped her feel better in this story by reminding her to breathe, exercise, and take some time for herself. When Parker did those things, she felt a lot better.

There are other things you can do too, like thinking of what makes you happy or taking some time to count to yourself, color, or listen to music. You might also want to talk to a trusted friend or adult about why you are feeling this way and what would help you feel better.

The next time you feel big emotions, try some of these things. Then think about how you feel afterward. Hopefully you'll feel better soon!

PARKER'S SLUMBER PARTY

My name is Parker.
I am having
a slumber party tonight!

Mom helps me decorate,
plan games,
and pick the perfect snacks.

My new friends, Nora and Isabella, arrive first.

"Come in!" I say. Ava and I help carry their things to my room.

The doorbell rings.
It is my surprise guest, Gia!
I introduce my bestie
to my new friends.

"Nice to meet you,"
says Gia.

"Hi, Gia!" says Nora.
"We will have so much fun tonight," says Isabella.

Mom puts out the snacks.
"Yum! Gummy worms!"
Ava cheers.

We make friendship bracelets.
I make a bracelet for each
one of my friends.

Next we play board games and build a pillow fort. "Parker, the pizza is here!" Ava calls.

We eat pizza
and have cupcakes
with sprinkles for dessert.

Outside the sun sinks lower. We play flashlight tag until Mom calls us in.

Soon we are in our pajamas, but no one is tired.
We are having too much fun.

We use my flashlights to make shadow puppets on the wall.

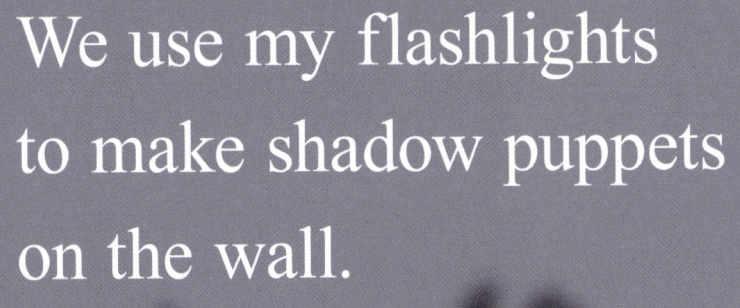

"What is that?"
Isabella asks.

"A little bird who will chirp the whole night," I whisper. "Then we can stay awake!" Gia and Nora giggle.

But Isabella and Ava
soon fall asleep.
After a while,
Nora starts to snore.
Then Gia drifts off.

I close my eyes for a minute.

When I open them,
it is morning!

We did not stay up all night, but we sure had fun trying!

FUN WITH FRIENDS

Parker loves spending time with her friends at slumber parties, playdates, and school. They have fun playing games and doing activities together. At the slumber party in this story, Parker and her friends played board games and flashlight tag, built a pillow fort, made friendship bracelets, and even created shadow puppets with their hands once the lights were out. Do you like any of the things that Parker and her friends did in this story? Are there other games and activities you and your friends love?

Have you ever had a slumber party with some of your friends? What games and activities would you plan for your slumber party? Do you think you would try to stay up all night?